DOCTOR CHANGE

JOANNA COLE

ILLUSTRATED BY

DONALD CARRICK

WILLIAM MORROW AND COMPANY, INC.
NEW YORK

Library of Congress Cataloging-in-Publication Data
Cole, Joanna.
Doctor Change.
Summary: A boy trapped in the service of a
magician discovers his master's secret of changing
shape and escapes from him three times with
the aid of a maiden.
[1. Fairy tales. 2. Folklore]
I. Carrick, Donald, ill.   II. Title.
PZ8.C6824Do 1986   [E] [398.2]   86-881
ISBN 0-688-06135-4
ISBN 0-688-06136-2 (lib. bdg.)

For my mother
—*J.C.*

For Nadine
—*D.C.*

Tom was a poor boy looking for work.

   He came to a town and walked around until he saw a house with a brass plate on the door and a sign in the window. On the brass plate were the words: DOCTOR CHANGE, and the sign said: BOY WANTED.

   "I could do worse than work for a doctor," thought Tom. "Maybe I'll learn something." He knocked twice.

The doctor came to the door. He was a heavy man with crooked little teeth. "What do you want?" he asked.

"I am looking for work," said Tom.

"Can you read?" asked the doctor.

"Yes," replied Tom. "I've been to school."

"Then I can't use you," growled the man, and shut the door.

Tom was puzzled, but he said to himself, "If that's the game, I know how to play." He walked to the end of town, turned his jacket inside out, and threw away his cap. Then he went back to the doctor's house.

"What do you want?" asked the man.

"I need work," said Tom.

"Can you read?" asked the doctor.

"No," said Tom. "I've never been to school."

"Good," said Doctor Change. "Come in and get started."

Doctor Change showed Tom all through the house. Then he led him to a small room right under the roof. All that was in it was a table, a chair, and a big leather book.

"You will sweep and scrub the rest of the house, but don't ever come into this room!" said Doctor Change.

Tom did as he was told. As for the doctor, every morning he went into the little room and didn't come out until nightfall.

One day, as Tom was sweeping outside the room, he bent over and peeked through the keyhole. There was the doctor, reading the big leather book.

Suddenly, Doctor Change was gone, and in his place Tom saw a cat. In the blink of an eye, the cat was replaced by a princess. Then the princess disappeared, and one after another Tom saw a hat, a vase of flowers, and a pair of shoes. The shoes stepped off the chair, and there was the doctor again.

"Now I know why he calls himself Doctor Change," thought Tom.

When Tom looked again, the doctor was eating a big steak. He ate all the meat. He licked the grease off the plate. Then he sat looking at the bone. Suddenly he became a dog and gnawed the bone till it was gone. Then the doctor returned to his own shape and began reading the book again.

"That's a hungry man," Tom said to himself.

Tom was amazed by what he saw, but he was frightened, too. He knocked on the door.

"What do you want?" asked Doctor Change.

"I want to leave your service," said Tom.

"See if you can," said the doctor, with a strange smile.

Tom grabbed his jacket and walked out the front door. There was Doctor Change standing in the path. Tom took a step, and suddenly the doctor was gone. In his place was an iron fence. Tom tried to go around it, but it just grew longer. He tried to climb over it, but it grew taller. At last, Tom went back in the house.

"A stupid boy like you can't get away from *me*," said Doctor Change.

The next day Doctor Change came downstairs with a trunk.

"I am going away on a trip," he said. "Make sure you do your work while I am gone."

Then the doctor closed the front door and rode away in a coach.

As soon as he was gone, Tom ran to the door. He turned the knob, but the door would not open. He tried the windows, but the shutters were locked tight.

When he saw he couldn't escape, Tom went up to the little room. That door was locked, too, but Tom soon found the key. Once inside, he opened the big leather book.

Day after day, Tom did nothing but read that book, which was full of the doctor's spells. Then he began to practice. At first, his spells didn't always work perfectly. But at last he could change as well as his master.

At the end of the month, Tom stood before the huge front door. He changed into a cat, but he couldn't squeeze under the door. He changed into a mouse, but he was still too big. Even an ant couldn't fit under that door. At last Tom changed into a puddle of water and *dripped* out onto the front step!

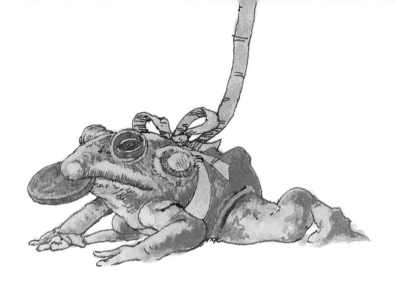

Then he resumed his own shape and went whistling out into the sunshine. He walked through the town and into the countryside.

Soon he saw a girl near a well. As he came closer, he could see that she was crying. "What's wrong?" asked Tom.

"I dropped a copper coin down the well," sobbed the girl. "It's all the money I have."

"Don't worry," said Tom. "I'll help you. When you see a frog, tie your ribbon around it and lower it into the well."

The girl, whose name was Kate, thought Tom was teasing her, but in a second, Tom was gone, and a little yellow frog sat before her on the grass. She tied her ribbon around it and lowered it into the well. When she pulled it up again, the frog had the coin in its mouth.

Then Tom appeared again. Kate was puzzled, so Tom explained about Doctor Change and his magic book. When Tom told how he had escaped as a puddle of water, Kate said, "I don't believe it!"

"Sit down and think about it, and you will," said Tom, and he turned into a chair. Kate's eyes opened wide in amazement, but the chair looked so comfortable that she had to sit. And the next thing, there she was on Tom's lap, laughing.

———————————

When Doctor Change returned to his house, he called for Tom. But of course Tom was nowhere to be found. Doctor Change was so angry that he set out to bring Tom back.

"Doctor Change is coming," Tom said to Kate. "Will you help me?"

"Of course," said Kate. "You helped me, didn't you?"

"Then remember, trust your ears, not your eyes," said Tom, and off he ran.

Kate kept walking. At the bend in the road she came upon a bucket of water, but Tom was not to be seen. Then Kate remembered Tom's story about changing into a puddle, and she felt sure he must be in the bucket. She tried to hide the bucket, but Doctor Change was clever.

"My throat is dry, Missy," he said. "I'll give you this gold coin for that water."

"I can't sell it," said Kate.

"I'll give you two coins," said Doctor Change.

"Never!" said Kate.

"Then I'll give you the whole purse," said the doctor.

Just then Kate heard a whisper, "Sell the water, but keep the bucket."

Kate took the purse and poured the water into a flask. Then Doctor Change returned home. "I told you before," he said to the flask, "you can't get away from me."

Kate hung the bucket on a branch and sat down to cry. All at once she heard Tom's voice. "Hey, get me down from here!"

"You were the bucket, not the water!" laughed Kate.

Doctor Change cast many spells to change the water back to Tom, but it *was* water and it *stayed* water.

Once again Tom saw Doctor Change coming and off he ran. Kate walked a little way, and she saw a yellow horse standing in the road.

When the doctor saw Kate patting the horse so tenderly, he said, "I'll give you two bags of gold for that horse, Missy."

Kate put her arms around the horse's neck and heard Tom's whisper again. "Sell the horse but keep the saddle."

And no sooner was the doctor out of sight when there was Tom. "You were the saddle, not the horse!" cried Kate.

This time when Tom saw the doctor storming along the road, he quickly turned himself into a ring on Kate's finger.

Doctor Change looked around for Tom. He saw no bucket, no horse, nothing on the road but Kate. Then he noticed the ring sparkling on her finger.

"That's no ring for a poor person like you," he said. "Let me buy it, Missy."

Kate put her hand to her ear, and again she heard the whisper. "Sell the ring, but do not put it in his hand."

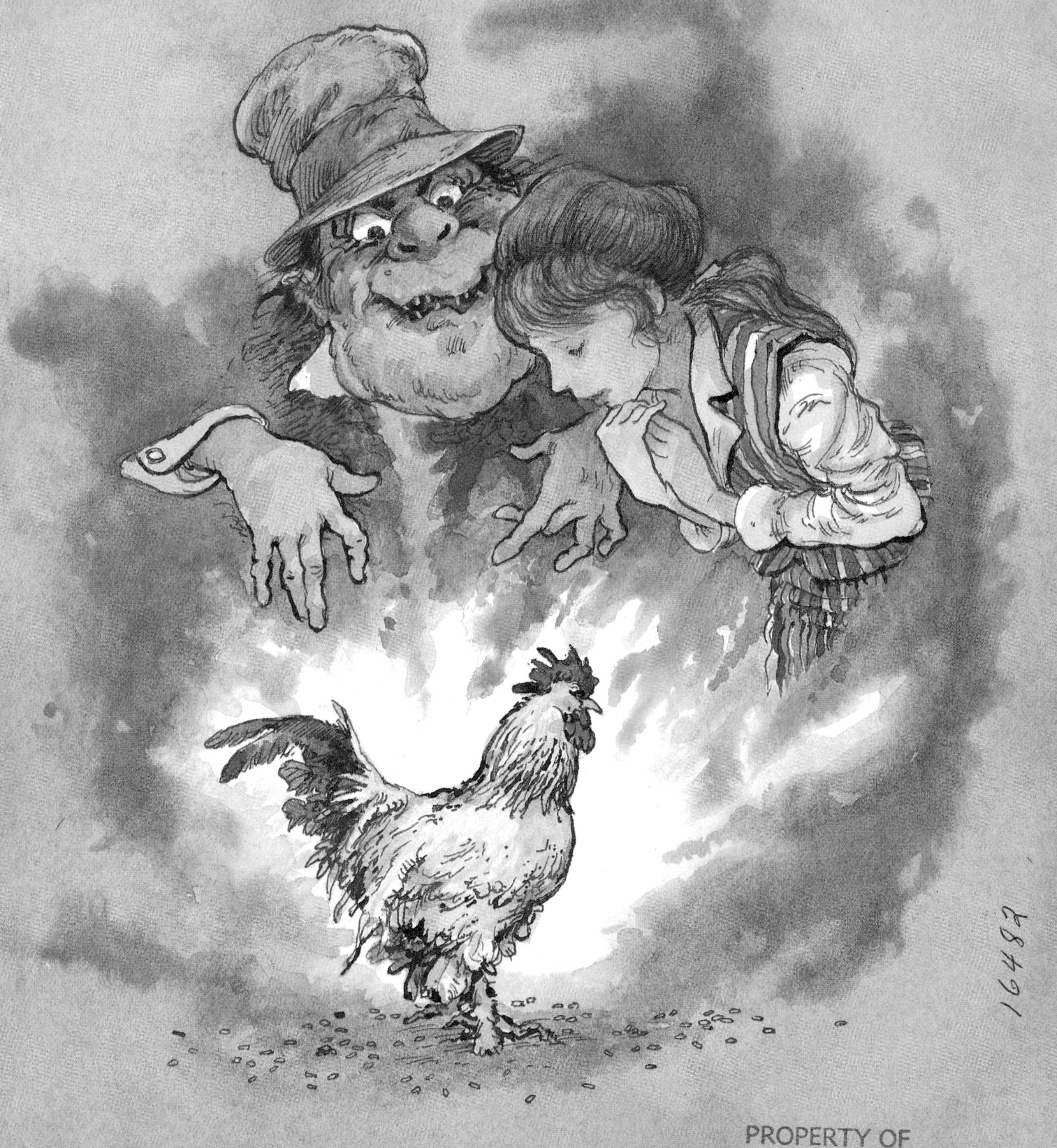

This time the greedy doctor gave Kate three bags of gold. She took off the ring and dropped it on the ground.

At once the ring broke into grains of rice. When Doctor Change saw the rice, he became a rooster and began pecking it up. But Tom changed from a grain of rice to a fox, and he ate the rooster, feathers and all. Then Tom returned to his own shape again. Kate was so glad to see him that she kissed him.

Tom and Kate had enough gold to buy a fine farm. They also had each other. Tom was so happy to be himself that he forgot all about changing into anyone or anything else.

But sometimes he did it to make the baby laugh.

DATE DUE

HIGHSMITH   #45102